D1523786

DIGGIN' IT

REAL ESTATE RESCUE COZY MYSTERIES,
BOOK 4

PATTI BENNING

SUMMER PRESCOTT BOOKS PUBLISHING

CHAPTER ONE

Flora Abner teetered on top of the ladder as she carefully slid the live trap into the shed's loft. It was already set, with a can of cat food inside. Using the cheap stuff to catch the persistent raccoon hadn't worked in the past, so today she was using a can of her own cat's food. It was a premium brand, and cost a pretty penny. She hoped the raccoon appreciated it. With any luck, it would be his last meal before he was evicted from her property for good.

She pushed the trap a little further into the loft, setting it right along the wall, where it would be easy for the raccoon to crawl inside. Once it was in place, she carefully made her way back down the ladder. Sure, the uneven shed floor might not be the safest place to have set the ladder up, but she was beyond frustrated. She and Grady, one of her new friends and someone who knew way more about home repairs than she did, had been working on her shed for a little over a week. They had gotten everything out of it and had covered the important items with a tarp near the house. There had been a lot of junk to pick through, things the previous owner had left behind. Some of it Grady had taken to sell at a scrap yard. The rest was piled by the road, waiting for the weekly trash pickup. She had a feeling her new garbageman wouldn't appreciate it, but she had called ahead to warn the garbage company, and she needed that stuff gone.

Empty, the little shed looked a lot more depressing. There were holes in the siding, one big, gaping hole in the roof, and the whole thing was leaning dangerously to one side. She tried to have faith that Grady knew what he was doing and the shed would look almost new by the end of summer, but privately she still thought knocking the whole thing down and starting fresh might be the better option.

The worst part was, the raccoon still hadn't moved out. She saw its beady little eyes on her security cameras every night. It was too smart for its own good, and had been plaguing her for months. She had even had to resort to using bungee straps to keep her garbage dumpster shut tight. She wished the creature would just move on. There were acres of perfectly good woods all around her; her shed couldn't be that much more comfortable for it to live in.

After folding the ladder and stashing it under the tarp near the back of her house, she put her hands on her hips and glared at the shed.

"You'd better take the bait this time," she muttered. "We'll find you a nice place to live, it just can't be here."

Then she sighed and turned back around, trying to decide what she should do with the rest of her day. She wasn't confident enough in her own skills to try to work on the shed without Grady, and he was at work. She had mown the lawn the week before, so she didn't need to do that again quite yet. She had been watching some videos about how to repair a hole in drywall, but she didn't quite feel ready to tackle the damaged ceiling in the upstairs bedroom where the roof had been leaking.

She decided she might as well go to town and buy some more mulch. She had been working on extending the flowerbeds a little, so they wrapped around the edges of the house. She liked the look of the flowers, and she had found that she enjoyed gardening as a hobby. She wasn't sure if she had a green thumb or if she was just lucky, but the flowers she planted a couple weeks ago were still doing well. More flowers could only be a good thing, right?

A few minutes later, after a quick goodbye to Amaretto, the fluffy white Persian cat who had Flora wrapped around her paw, she was on her way into town. Warbler, Kentucky, was like nowhere she had ever lived before, but even after living here for most of the summer, her enjoyment of the quaint, small-town feel hadn't worn off. She probably would have found it claustrophobic if she had grown up here, but coming from a big city, the small-town experience was nice. It was like taking a step back, and finally getting a peek at another world. One she had always known existed, but had never had the chance to experience.

The town was simple to navigate. There were two main streets, which crossed in the middle of Warbler, and it was along these two streets that most of the businesses were located. She did most of her shopping here, and even though the small businesses didn't always have the selection she was used to in bigger, chain stores, getting to know the owners and employees made up for it. It felt good to give her money to local families instead of some big corporation, even if it was a little less convenient at times.

On her way to the nursery where she had taken to buying most of her gardening supplies, she stopped by Violet Delights, the coffee shop owned by one of her best friends in town. She had tried most of their drinks, but always went back to her favorite. Violet, the coffee shop's owner, nodded at her when she came in. There was one other woman at the counter waiting for her drink to be made, so Flora stepped into line beside her.

"Hey," Violet said. "I'll be right with you. You want your regular?"

Flora nodded. The woman she didn't know glanced over at her. "What do you usually get?" she asked. "I don't drink a lot of coffee, and I never know what to order so I usually stick with the basics."

"I usually get the white-chocolate caramel latte," Flora told her. "But I've liked every drink I've tried."

The woman, a blonde with makeup that Flora was jealous of, wrinkled her nose. "It sounds too sweet for me."

"We can make it less sweet," Violet said as she handed an iced coffee over to the woman. "Here you go."

"Thanks." The woman paused to get a straw and some napkins while Violet turned to Flora.

"Doing some shopping while you're in town?" her friend asked.

"I need more mulch from the nursery," Flora said, watching as Violet began to make her latte. "I really should have had someone deliver a truckload of it, but I keep thinking I just need a few more bags."

"Remember it for next year. Get someone to deliver some in the spring, and you won't have to keep running into town like this."

"I'll make a note," Flora said as the blonde woman left the store. She was learning a lot about being a homeowner, and while this first year she was going to chalk up to one big learning experience, she wanted to be better prepared for next year.

She paid for her coffee, thanked Violet, and left with the latte in her hand. She sipped it as she drove to the nursery, and sat in the parking lot while she finished it. She wasn't in any real hurry, and it was nice to just relax and take the day in.

Once she drained the last dregs of her coffee, she grabbed her purse and the empty cup and got out of her truck. There wasn't a trashcan in front of the nursery, but there was a dumpster around the side of it, and she didn't think they would care very much if her little coffee cup made its way inside. She eyed the bags of mulch sitting out front as she walked, wondering how many she should get. They never seemed to go as far as she expected them to, so she doubled her original estimation of five bags to ten. Even if it was too many, she could always just store the extra for later.

She moved her purse over her elbow as she stepped around the building and lifted the top of the big dumpster with one hand, tossing her coffee cup in. Just as she was letting the top drop shut, a rough hand grabbed her by the shoulder and pulled her back. Another hand covered her mouth. She had a moment to register that the hand over her mouth was wearing a thick leather glove before a gravelly voice growled in her ear, "Drop your purse and then walk away without looking back. If you make a scene, you'll regret it."

Flora froze. Was she getting mugged? That had never happened to her before, not even when she lived in Chicago. Here, in Warbler of all places?

For a second she thought about trying to fight back. Maybe she could stomp on the man's foot, or smash the back of her head into his face.

Then she realized it wasn't worth it. It wasn't like she was going to be able to knock him out in one hit, and she could tell by the strength of his hands and how tall he felt from where he was pressed to her back, that he was a lot bigger than her. Fighting back wouldn't achieve anything but to increase the possibility of her being injured or even killed. Shakily, she extended the arm that the purse was looped over and it fell to the ground with a thud. The man released her, but moved the hand that had been covering her mouth to the back of her neck.

"Walk into the store. Say whatever you want, I'll be gone before the police get here. Remember, don't look back."

She had no way of knowing if the man had a gun or a knife, so she just did what he told her to, her feet scuffing the ground as she walked stiffly away from him and back around the building. After a moment she heard the sound of running footsteps fading away. Only when she had reached the corner of the building did she risk a glance back, but the space near the dumpster was empty. Her purse was gone, and so was the man who had assaulted her.

Feeling dizzy with shock, fear, and adrenaline, Flora stumbled into the nursery. All she could think was that she wanted to call the police... and that she hoped she hadn't kept anything irreplaceable inside her purse.

CHAPTER TWO

"Show me where you were standing when the assailant attacked you."

Flora shuffled so she was in front of the dumpster, one hand extended as if she was lifting the lid. Officer Hendricks had made it to the nursery in only about twenty minutes, and Ms. Michaels, the kind older woman who owned the nursery, had helpfully offered Flora a stool and a glass of water when she saw the state Flora was in, and had sat with her until he arrived. Ms. Michaels had been horrified to hear that Flora had been mugged on the nursery's property, and somehow Flora found herself comforting the older woman and promising her that it wasn't their fault at all.

It helped, in a weird way. It gave her something to focus on other than her own erratic thoughts. Seeing Officer Hendricks pull into the parking lot in his police cruiser had been another grounding moment. She was glad he was here, even if she wasn't thrilled at having to reenact the crime.

"Tell me what he said to you, word for word," Officer Hendricks said, standing back far enough to keep an eye on the entire side of the nursery building. He wasn't looking at Flora anymore; instead he seemed to be sweeping the ground for clues.

Flora repeated the words as well as she could, then added, "His voice was low and a little weird, like he was trying to disguise how he sounded."

"Do you think he's someone you know?" Officer Hendricks asked.

Flora frowned. "I doubt it. I don't know that many people, and he didn't seem familiar otherwise." She narrowed her eyes. "And before you say it, no, it wasn't Grady."

Officer Hendricks raised his hands. "Whoa, easy. I wasn't going to suggest it was. I can admit I was a little unfair to him in the past, but from everything

I've seen, he seems like a real friend to you. I'm more concerned that it might be someone who followed you here. Where did you go before this? Who did you tell you were coming here?"

"The only other place I stopped was the coffee shop, and the only person who knew I was coming here was Violet. I don't think anyone's been following me. Why would they? Why mug me? It's not like I'm known for carrying a ton of cash around, and I don't have fancy jewelry or anything."

"I'm just covering all the bases," Officer Hendricks said. He sighed and looked around again. "No security cameras out here, of course. You said he ran the opposite direction, away from the parking lot. The other side of the block is a residential area. I'll go knock on some doors and see if anyone saw anything. In the meantime, I need you to write out a list of everything you had in the purse, along with a description of your purse, and bring it to the police station. If you have pictures of any items, that would be helpful."

"Do you think I'll get any of it back?"

"It's possible. Often, in situations like these, we will find the purse and its contents dropped somewhere or disposed of in a garbage receptacle, with the contents of the wallet missing. Sometimes the perpetrator tries to sell more valuable items at a pawn shop or online, which is why the description is helpful. We can keep an eye out for those. The very first thing you should focus on is canceling all of your cards and alerting your bank to the loss of your wallet. I hope you weren't carrying around much cash, because chances of you getting that back are infinitesimal."

"Only about forty dollars," she said. "But... everything else is in there. Everything except my phone." She had gotten into the habit of keeping *that* in the back pocket of her jeans, since she liked to carry it around with her while she was working on the house. "I don't even have my truck keys on me. I'm going to need to get a ride home. I have spares there, at least."

"I'll have one of the other officers give you a ride," he told her. "Get on canceling those cards first thing. You can figure everything else out later. And Ms. Abner? You did the right thing, by handing over your purse. It wasn't worth getting hurt over."

She took a deep breath. "Thanks. It helps, but I've got to admit I am starting to feel pretty mad at that guy now that the shock is wearing off. I can't believe I was actually mugged! Has it happened to anyone else?"

"We haven't had any reports yet," he told her.

She grimaced. Of course something like this would happen to her and only her. She was just grateful that Officer Hendricks was professional enough not to point out her continuing string of bad luck. With a sigh, she thanked him for his help, wished him luck in tracking down the person who had mugged her, and then set her mind to figuring out how on earth she was going to replace her credit cards, her bank cards, and her driver's license, all without any form of ID.

The officer who gave her a ride home was a woman a few years younger than Flora. She was kind and talk-ative, and as a result Flora was feeling a little better when she got back to her house and said goodbye to the other woman.

At least, until she realized she didn't have her house keys either.

She stared at her very firmly locked front door for a long, long moment before she sat down on the porch step with her head in her hands and groaned.

How was she supposed to get into her house? She had foolishly assured the officer who drove her home that she would be fine, and the woman was already long gone. Her extra set of truck keys was inside, but that didn't do her any good, seeing as how she couldn't get to them, and her truck was still in town.

She really hadn't thought this through.

After a few minutes of feeling bad for herself, she got back to her feet and started trying the windows and then the back door. She wasn't surprised to find they were all locked. She was careful about security, and it was coming back to bite her now.

She was behind the house when her eyes fell on the edge of the ladder, which was just peeking out from under the tarp. She looked from the ladder to one of the second-floor windows. An open second floor window. The second story of her house got sweltering under the summer sun, so she had taken to leaving the upper story bedroom windows open during the day.

Climbing in through one of them seemed like a terrible idea, but also seemed like the only idea that would get her into her house in any reasonable amount of time.

After extending the ladder to its tallest height and triple checking that it was as stable as it was going to get, Flora carefully climbed up to the top of it. There was a screen in the window, but frankly, she was past caring right now. She had taken the gardening trowel from under the tarp and used it to cut through the screen, and then found the latches by feel. She pulled the screen away from the window, then slipped it inside and got off the ladder to reposition it so she could climb through the window more easily.

It wasn't easy or pretty, and she nearly fell twice, but finally she slid to the floor in the unused upper bedroom and just laid there for a second, panting and ready to be done with this day.

The look on her cat's face when she came downstairs almost made up for it. Amaretto stared at her with wide eyes, and then darted away, like she had seen a ghost.

"You didn't even hear me breaking in upstairs," Flora called after her. "Some watch-cat you are."

Grumbling to herself, Flora found her spare keys and then poured herself a glass of lemonade. While she drank it at the kitchen table, she considered her options.

She needed a ride back into town. She knew Violet and Grady were both at work, but she wasn't as sure of Sydney's schedule, so she tried calling his cell phone. It rang through to voicemail. She tried calling the feed store instead, and heard his familiar voice answer.

"Hey, Sydney," she said once he got done with his introductory spiel. "It's Flora. I hate to ask, but when do you get out of work?"

He paused. "In about an hour. Why? Is everything okay?"

She didn't want to get into the mugging right now. "It's a long story, but is there any way you can swing by my place, pick me up, and take me into town so I can get my truck? I'll tell you everything on the way, and I'll buy you a pizza or something as thanks."

"Sure," he said, still sounding confused. "I'm happy to help, and I'm going to hold you to that story. It sounds like an interesting one."

She thanked him and ended the call, then turned her focus to canceling all of her stolen cards. It took longer than she expected, and she was still on the phone with the bank when Sydney showed up at her house just over an hour later. She grabbed her truck keys, felt briefly naked without her purse, then hurried outside, waving at him and pointing at the phone in her hand as an explanation for why she wasn't talking.

She finally managed to get off the call with her account manager just as they were pulling into town. Sydney had waited with commendable patience while she talked, but now he looked at her eagerly and she grimaced.

"Right…" she said. "Storytime."

CHAPTER THREE

When Flora woke up the next morning, it took her a few minutes to remember why she felt so unhappy. Then the memory of the mugging the day before came back to her and she grimaced. Moving Amaretto carefully off her stomach, she sat up and grabbed her phone from the bedside table. The security cameras had the usual footage of the annoying raccoon going into her shed. She scowled at it for a second, then checked her messages. She didn't have any missed calls or voicemails from the police station, which was disappointing. It would be nice if the police managed to find her purse and it somehow, miraculously had her driver's license in it, but she knew better than to hold her breath. After getting back home in her truck the day before, she had found the documents she would need to get a replacement, but she hadn't had time to actually do it before the DMV closed for the day.

She got up and started getting ready for the day when a horrible thought made her pause.

She needed to get a new driver's license, but they weren't free, and until the bank mailed her replacement cards, she had no money. She couldn't even go into the bank to get a card the same day, because her bank was located in Chicago. It had a few branches around the Midwest, but none as far as Kentucky. It hadn't been much of an issue before, since she could do everything she needed to online, but right now she was regretting her choices.

"This is the worst week ever," she decided as she yanked her shirt down over her head and stomped out into the living room. Amaretto followed her, winding around her ankles and almost making her trip. Flora stumbled into the kitchen to get the cat her food, then started the coffee maker and flopped down at the kitchen table while she waited for it to make her morning drink.

She needed a new driver's license as soon as possible. Technically, she probably shouldn't even drive to the DMV without one. She hadn't even been thinking of that when she drove her truck home yesterday. But how was she supposed to get there without driving? Warbler didn't exactly have a taxi service.

Even if it did, she didn't have the money to pay for it.

Groaning, she let her head fall to the table. She really must have been out of it yesterday. She hadn't thought of any of this until now. The day was a blur to her. She hadn't realized until now just how deeply the mugging had shocked her.

She took a deep breath. "Okay, I can figure this out," she said. "I have friends. I could call Sydney again." She knew Violet would be at work, and Grady didn't have a cell phone. Her neighbor, Beth York, would probably be happy to give her a ride into town, but the older woman didn't have a car.

Sydney it was. If he was working, she would call the hardware store and see if Grady could come over after his shift.

She picked up her cell phone, but before she could even touch the screen, it lit up. She blinked at the sight of Grady's number on the caller ID. It was like she had somehow summoned him just by thinking about him.

A second later, she remembered that he wasn't working today. She had gotten off track – he had today off and they were supposed to work on the shed together in a couple of hours.

Relieved, she answered the call.

"Hey, Grady," she said. "I'm glad you called. Can you do me a favor?"

"If it's about coffee, that's what I'm calling you about. You want me to pick up a latte for you on my way over?"

"Actually, I need a ride somewhere. I need to go to the DMV, but I don't have my driver's license. We can stop at Violet Delights on our way."

"Why don't you have your driver's license?" he asked, sounding befuddled.

"It's a long story," she said. "I'll tell you on the way into town."

Grady picked her up twenty minutes later. She still felt frazzled and unsure of herself, but the sight of him pulling up in his familiar truck relaxed something inside of her. She hadn't even been aware of how jumpy she was until she stepped outside and relaxed when she saw him.

"Hey," she said, her voice sounding fake-cheerful even to her own ears. "Thanks for giving me a ride."

He gave her look like she was being weird, which she probably was. "I have no idea what's going on," he admitted. "Hop in and tell me about it."

She slid into the passenger seat and buckled her seatbelt as he backed the truck out of her driveway. "Well, like I said, I need to go to the DMV because I don't have my driver's license. Or my wallet. I need to remember to ask Violet if I can borrow some money when we stop by the coffee shop."

"And, why don't you have your driver's license or your wallet? Did you lose your purse?" he asked, sounding utterly puzzled.

She fidgeted. It hadn't been so hard telling Sydney what happened, probably because she was still somewhat in shock. Telling Grady would just make it more real.

She had to tell him, though. She'd have to tell Violet too, she knew. There was no point in putting it off, not with how quickly word spread in this town where everyone knew everyone.

"I was mugged," she admitted in a quiet voice. "Yesterday, when I went to buy more mulch. He got my purse. I wasn't hurt or anything, and I reported it to the police, but they didn't catch the guy. I'll probably never see my purse or anything in it again."

Grady turned his head to stare at her until he remembered he was driving and forced his attention back to the road.

"You sure you're okay?" he asked.

She breathed out. "Yeah. It was just, well, it was pretty terrifying."

He nodded, his jaw clenched. "You should've called me."

"One of the other police officers gave me a ride home," she said. "I wasn't thinking clearly for most of the day. I think I was in shock. Plus, you're hard to get a hold of." She nudged him with her elbow. "You don't have a cell phone."

He grumbled, "Maybe I should get one."

She smiled, glad he wasn't really mad at her for not calling him sooner. She figured she would be a little offended too, if one of her closest friends had something like that happen and didn't tell her about it. Violet was going to freak out, but for some reason, she was less worried about Violet's reaction than Grady's.

"You have all the papers you need?" he asked after a moment. "For your new license."

She nodded. "Yeah. Thankfully, I knew right where my birth certificate was, and I have mail with my address on it. I brought my Social Security card too, just in case they need that. Hopefully I don't get mugged again right now. That would be really bad." She gave a weak laugh. It was a poor attempt at a joke, but it felt better than dwelling on it.

They reached Violet Delights and went into the coffee shop together, leaving Grady's truck parked out front. Violet greeted them with her usual wave, but the cheerful grin that was always on her face was missing. Flora wondered if Sydney had told her about the mugging. It made sense – the two of them seemed to talk quite a lot now that Sydney was part of their little group.

"Hey," Violet said as they approached the counter. "Your regulars?"

At their nods, she started working on the drinks. She glanced around, then lowered her voice. "Did you two hear what happened last night?"

Flora blinked, confused. She had been certain Violet was about to ask about the mugging, but her phrasing was off. Flora wouldn't need to have *heard* about it, since it had happened to her. She and Grady traded a clueless look.

"No?" Flora said slowly. "I don't think we did."

Violet's eyes widened. "It's horrible. A man was attacked and killed on his way home from work last night. People have been talking about it all morning. The consensus seems to be it was a mugging gone wrong."

Beside her, Grady tensed. She could practically feel his gaze burning into the side of her head, but she kept her focus on Violet.

"Who was he? Anyone we knew?"

Violet shook her head. "Someone named Ethan Alberry. I checked online and his face is plastered all over social media. I think I might have spotted him in here once or twice, but he wasn't a regular and I didn't know him outside of that."

"I think I know his wife," Grady said, to Flora's surprise. "Or ex-wife. My boss is her father, and she lives across the street from the hardware store. She comes in to talk to him a lot, and I remember hearing more than I wanted to about their divorce. Ethan stopped in a few times too, before it was all finalized. I felt bad for the guy."

"I'm going to move my car around to the front of the building before it gets dark out," Violet said with a shudder. "I don't feel safe walking around town by myself until they catch the guy. You two be careful, okay?"

Flora hesitated. Now seemed like a good time to tell Violet what happened. It would just be weird to bring it up later.

"Weird coincidence..." she said with an awkward grin. "I was mugged yesterday too. Thank goodness all he got away with was my purse. I'm starting to realize how lucky I was."

Violet stared at her, slowly put the coffee cup down on the counter, and reached out to gently shake Flora's shoulder.

"You were mugged yesterday and I'm just hearing about it now? Are you insane, girl? Why didn't you call me? Are you sure you're all right? He didn't hurt you?"

"I'm sorry," Flora said, wincing. "I just wasn't thinking clearly yesterday, okay? I already heard it from Grady. The next time something horrible happens to me, the two of you will be the first to know."

"Oh my goodness," Violet said, putting her hands to her temples. "Your life stresses me out, Flora. You don't think it's the same guy, do you? Oh, what am I saying? There can't be *that* many muggers in town."

Delayed fear made Flora's stomach turn sour. She really could have died, couldn't she have? It seemed she had made the right decision not to try to fight back, but the thought of how easily things could have gone differently terrified her.

CHAPTER FOUR

Flora cradled her temporary driver's license like it was the most precious thing she owned. In a way, it was. She hadn't been aware of how reliant she was on it until she lost it. She could legally drive again. Granted, she didn't have any money for gas or groceries, but that was a temporary problem. Holding onto the temporary driver's license, she finally believed that everything would end up being all right. She was still recovering from her near brush with death, but she *would* recover. That was the important thing.

"Do you want to stop anywhere else?" Grady offered as he drove them back through town.

"No," she said with a sigh. "I don't have anything else I need to do." Especially without a way to pay for anything, but she didn't want to mention that, because Grady would probably offer to do something silly, like pay for her groceries for her.

"Do you still want to work on the shed today?" he asked.

"Yeah. I could use something normal to keep my mind occupied." She frowned. "I wanted to keep extending the flower beds, but I never did get my mulch. That jerk really wrecked my day."

She felt guilty as soon as the words were out of her mouth. He — and she *knew* it was the same person, because Warbler was tiny and coincidences like that just didn't happen — had gone on to kill a man later that same day. She had gotten off lucky, and someone else had lost their life. She shouldn't joke about that.

"Let's go get some," Grady said, putting on the blinker to turn toward the nursery. "It'll give you something to do tomorrow, while I'm at work."

"No money, Grady," she said, gesturing at her empty lap, where her purse would normally sit. "I'm flat broke until the mail gets my new cards here."

"You can pay me back," he told her. "But we're getting that mulch."

She bit back her initial inclination to argue, and relaxed back into the seat instead. "Thanks, Grady. I appreciate it."

All of her relaxation fled her when Grady pulled into the nursery's parking lot. She tensed, staring at the dumpster, which was just visible around the corner. It was ridiculous to be afraid of coming back here, especially with Grady by her side, but her pounding heart didn't seem to care how rational its reaction was.

"You okay?" Grady asked, giving her a concerned look. He seemed to be doing that a lot lately.

She forced herself to smile. "Yeah. I'm fine. Let's head in. I was going to get ten bags. Is that okay?"

"Sure. You should just have it delivered next year, though. Cheaper that way."

"You sound just like Violet," she said, giving a roll of her eyes that was only a little forced. "I'll try to remember."

She unbuckled her seatbelt and slipped out of the truck. It was an overcast, humid day, and she could smell the flowers inside the building from here. She wished the lingering tension inside her chest would go away so she could enjoy it.

"Let's go," she said, striding toward the building. "Mulch awaits us."

Ms. Michaels was sitting behind the counter when Flora walked inside. She was working on some knitting, but looked up when the bell over the door jingled. Her eyes widened when she saw Flora, and she dropped the knitting to the counter.

"Dear, I wasn't expecting to see you again so soon," she said. "Please, let me apologize again—"

"Really, you don't need to," Flora assured her. "What happened wasn't your fault. I don't blame you or anyone who works here at all."

"I still feel terrible. I'm glad you're still willing to shop here." She sighed. "Business just isn't what it used to be. We've had to let someone go recently, though that decision was helped along by his own actions. Every customer is precious now."

Flora's heart sank at the words. "You're not going out of business, are you?"

"Only time will tell. Maybe it would be better if we did, even if just temporarily. Finn ran out of second chances last week – you know how his temper was – and with him gone, it's just me, Amy, and Bella working here now. With just us girls, I'm not sure if we're safe, not after your attack and hearing about what happened to that poor man yesterday as well. This town just isn't what it used to be, and if the man who attacked you comes back, I'm afraid of what would happen."

She remembered Finn — he was a surly man who had reluctantly helped her load mulch into her truck a few times. She felt bad that he had lost his job, but she felt worse that the few remaining employees might face the same thing.

"Well, I've still got a lot of work to do around my house, so I'll try my best to keep you in business single-handedly."

The older woman gave her a kind but sad smile. "I appreciate the sentiment, dear. What can I help you with today?"

Flora put in her order for ten bags of brown mulch and watched while she typed the order into the ancient computer. When Grady went to pay, she waved him away.

"I still feel bad about yesterday," she said, looking at Flora. "The mulch is on us today."

"But… you just said you were worried you might go out of business," Flora said. "I can't accept this."

"You don't have a choice," the older woman said. "The price of the mulch won't make or break us. Please, dear. Let me do this for my own conscience."

Flora bit her lip. "Well, okay, if you're sure…"

The woman patted her hand. "Go on, dear. I'm sorry we don't have anyone to help you load it up this time, but it looks like you've got it covered. I hope we'll see you again soon. And be careful. This town isn't as safe as it used to be."

With that ominous warning in her ears, she thanked the other woman one last time and turned toward the door. Grady reached it first and opened it for her, but before she could go through, another man walked in. He was huge, taking up almost the whole door, and all muscle, with shortly cropped black hair. Flora stepped back to let him go by, but he paused partway through and glanced at Grady.

"Do you work here? I'm looking for a job."

"Sorry, man," Grady said. "I don't."

"They just had to let some people go," Flora told him. "I doubt they're hiring."

"Darn," he said, slumping. "Nowhere in town is hiring."

"You're not from around here, are you?" Flora asked. His accent gave him away — he sounded like he was from the Midwest, like she was. Before he could answer, she gasped. "Oh my goodness, I sound like some small-town person from the movies. I didn't mean it like that, it's just that I'm new here too."

He chuckled. "It's all right. Yeah, I moved here a couple weeks ago with a job offer that dried up before I even started." He shook her hand. "I'm Linus Kade. Nice to meet ya both."

"You too," Flora said. "Sorry things aren't working out so well for you. I'm sure you'll find a job soon. Someone has got to be hiring. I can ask around if you want."

"Really? I'd appreciate it. The only other person I know in town is my cousin. Can we exchange numbers?"

She nodded, and they made the trade. She was happy to help out a fellow newcomer to town, and hoped Violet might have some leads on who was hiring.

With that thought on her mind, she followed Grady outside and waited by the bags of mulch while he backed his truck up to them. Another pickup truck was sitting at the far end of the lot, the windshield facing the building. She spotted short, brown hair and a permanently grumpy face – Finn. It was weird seeing him right after Ms. Michaels had brought him up. She wondered if he was here to try to get his job back.

But then he started the truck and pulled out of the parking space, cutting Grady off with a plume of diesel smoke as he sped out of the lot. Coughing, she glared after him.

He didn't seem thrilled with having lost his job. She was just glad she wasn't here alone. She didn't like Finn, and just a day after the attack, the last thing she needed was another confrontation with an angry man.

CHAPTER FIVE

Working on the shed with Grady was a nice return to normalcy that she needed. Even checking the loft and finding the live trap was empty didn't irritate her as much as it normally did. The raccoon was out of sight, either hiding in the rafters or spending the day snoozing in the forest. She *might* be starting to feel a little bad at the fact that they were kicking the little guy out of his home, but there were plenty of other places he could live. She wanted a nice, clean, animal-proof shed to store her things in and she was going to get one, darn it.

Grady seemed reluctant to leave that evening, but she assured him she would be fine. She felt safe here, at her house with Amaretto meowing for her dinner and Beth just down the road. She was glad she had gotten returning to the scene of her attack out of the way early. It had helped, though the knowledge that the same person who attacked her had *killed* a man still made her feel uneasy. She hoped the police would catch the culprit soon.

She made sure her doors and windows were all locked tightly before she went to bed that night — even the upstairs ones, just in case someone got the same bright idea she'd had and used her ladder to sneak in. A part of her was worried she would have nightmares, but as soon as her head hit the pillow, she felt sleep tugging her under, and didn't remember a single one of her dreams until morning.

A cheery chime from her cell phone woke her up. Amaretto was purring on the pillow next to her head, and sunlight streamed in through the sheer curtains on her window. She laid still for a few moments, enjoying the relaxed feeling of having gotten the perfect amount of sleep, and not having any pressing commitments. Then, her phone chimed again.

She sat up, muffled a yawn, and reached for the device. Violet was the one who was texting her. Flora rubbed her eyes and squinted at the phone.

Emma asked if she could pick up an extra shift, so I'm free this afternoon. Want me to come over?

The second one read, *I'll get sandwiches from the sub place for us for lunch.*

All of that sounded great to Flora. She had food here — cans of vegetables and tuna, boxes of pasta, some frozen meals — but without her cards she couldn't buy anything fresh. She was planning on gardening today, but Violet could help her with that, and if she didn't want to, well, it wouldn't kill Flora to take an afternoon off and just hang out with her friend.

So she replied, *Yes, please!* with a lot of hearts and smiley faces following after it.

Then she turned to her purring cat. "Up and at 'em, lazy bones. It's breakfast time."

While Amaretto ate her fancy food — Flora was glad she had stocked up on it the previous weekend, because the cat would *not* be happy if they ran out — she ate some cereal with the last of her milk. It felt *weird* not to be able to just run out to the store and get more. She wasn't *rich*, but she'd had a well-paying job before this and she had enough savings now that she could live comfortably, especially since she had bought the house outright with the money her aunt had lent her. Not having access to her money was temporary, but it opened her eyes to how a lot of other people lived. She didn't know how successful her house-flipping career would be, but she swore to herself that she would make a point of donating to charities — *good* charities — when she could.

No one should have to wonder when they would be able to go out and buy milk again.

She got to work on the garden after that, hauling bags of mulch out to cover the soft soil when she was done weeding. It was hard, sweaty work, but it was satisfying. She only took a break when Violet texted her to ask what sort of sandwich she wanted. After a quick shower, she whipped up a fresh pitcher of lemonade and sat on her porch with a glass to wait for her friend.

When Violet pulled up and got out of her car, clutching a sandwich bag, Flora hurried down the porch steps to greet her with a hug. Violet and Grady were her two best friends here in Warbler — maybe anywhere, if she thought about it. She had kept in touch with her friends in Chicago, but between the distance and their busy lives, keeping in touch was as far as it went. Violet and Grady were *here*, and she saw them almost every day. They knew what she had been through, and had seen her at her worst and her best. She might have only known them for a few months, but those months had changed her in a way all the years since college hadn't.

"Every time I come over, this place looks better and better," Violet said, taking a moment to admire the house before she followed Flora up to the porch. "What are you working on today?"

"I spent the morning gardening," Flora said. "I never thought I would enjoy it as much as I do."

"Did you finish with the shed?" Violet sat down on one of the rocking chairs and put the bag of sandwiches on the little table between them. She took the wrapped parcels out and checked the labels before handing Flora one and keeping the other for herself.

"No, it's going to be a big project. We reinforced two of the supports yesterday, which was a pain since we had to mix concrete and join the new support to the old one. We'll probably finish the rest next week, and then we've still got to do the siding and the roof. And that's not even taking into account the floor. It's just dirt right now, and we've got to even it out and then lay a proper floor down."

"You sound less than thrilled," Violet said with a laugh. "I thought you enjoyed all of this DIY stuff."

"I enjoy working on the *house*. The shed is just a pain, but Grady is right that I need *somewhere* to store all of my tools, and fixing it up will be cheaper and easier than knocking it down and building a new one." She sighed. "I'll be glad when it's done and I don't mind the actual work, I just feel like I'm wasting time, you know?"

"You've still got, what, a year and a half? You'll be fine," Violet said. "I don't think you'll have any problems flipping this place."

"I don't know about that," Flora said, taking a bite of her sandwich. It was good, and she took a moment to enjoy the artfully assembled meal before continuing. "It seems like Warbler is on a decline. I talked to that lady from the plant nursery, and she had to let an employee go. And I met another newcomer to town, and he's having trouble finding a job at all."

"Darn, who did she let go? I'm friends with some of the girls who work there. They haven't mentioned anything."

"Ah, a guy named Finn. Kind of a grumpy guy, with brown hair?"

"I know him," Violet said. "He used to work for me a few years ago, actually. I think he's worked at most places in town by now, and he has a bad reputation for a reason. He's a jerk. I fired him when he went off on a customer because they complained that he gave them the wrong drink."

"Oh." Flora frowned, remembering Finn's angry departure from the nursery. Officer Hendricks had put forward the idea that her assailant was someone she knew, by which she thought he meant one of her friends, but maybe it *was* someone she knew... just not someone she knew very well. A disgruntled ex-employee could very well have been the one who attacked her outside the nursery.

"What's up? You look like something's bothering you."

"I'm just wondering if he's who attacked me. Finn. I mean, he was fired from his job, which must have made him angry. He was lurking right beside the building when I went with Grady to buy the mulch. Maybe he was trying to get revenge? And if he was just fired and has a bad reputation with the other businesses around town, maybe he really needed the money, so when the mugging worked with me, he went on to mug and kill that other guy. Ethan, or whatever his name was."

"Maybe." Violet frowned. "It's hard to believe he's a *murderer,* though. He had a bad temperament, but he worked for me for *months.* Besides, I asked around a little after that conversation with you and Grady, and it turns out one of my friends works with Ethan Alberry's ex-wife, Phoebe Brant. She *hated* him. I mean, really hated. She told my friend she hoped he ended up dead, and apparently was looking into appealing the court decision not to give her alimony in their divorce. It makes me wonder if she did it, or hired someone to do it and make it just look like a mugging."

Flora made a considering sound as she took another bite of her sandwich. A part of her hoped the person who mugged her wasn't the same person who killed

Ethan. Thinking about how close she came to dying made the whole experience seem more frightening.

On the other hand, if the incidents were unrelated, then it meant there were *two* violent criminals running around town, which meant her chances of running into one of them doubled.

CHAPTER SIX

Her new bank card arrived on Monday. Slipping it into her wallet felt like getting her life back. She and Grady had worked on the shed over the weekend, and she had finished extending the flowerbeds, but other than that, it had been an unusually quiet weekend for her. She was running low on gas in her truck, and didn't want to ask to borrow more money from her friends, so she had stuck to her house for the past few days.

Now, she desperately needed to go shopping. With a relieved sigh, she slipped her shoes on, grabbed her purse, and blew a goodbye kiss to Amaretto where the cat was napping on the back of the couch.

"I'll be back soon, princess," she said. "Guard the house while I'm gone."

It felt good to be behind the wheel again. Her first stop in town was the gas station. She waited by the pump while her gas tank filled up, trying to ignore how jumpy she felt whenever someone walked past behind her. She told herself she was being paranoid, but it was hard to ignore the fact that the mugger and whoever had killed Ethan, if they weren't the same person, were both still at large.

A little bit of paranoia was probably justified.

She hadn't eaten anything since a single fried egg for breakfast, so by the time she finished getting gas, her stomach was rumbling. She tried to avoid going grocery shopping on an empty stomach, because it led to her buying a lot of unhealthy food she didn't need. She decided to grab lunch before going to the grocery store, and drove to the same sandwich shop Violet had bought sandwiches from a few days ago. It was a little deli a single turn off of Main Street. The roof was a bright, lime green, and the wooden siding of the building was painted yellow. Though eye-watering, the little business looked cheerful, and Flora was already thinking of what she wanted to order as she stepped inside.

They made very good BLTs, but she also loved their honey roasted turkey breast. She got into line and peered at the menu, checking out the handful of new options. The owner of the sandwich shop came up with one or two new sandwich offerings every week. Today, the apple and walnut chicken salad sandwich caught her eye. It sounded fresh, somewhat healthy, and delicious.

"Oh hey, it's you again."

She blinked and turned to look at the person she was standing next to. It took her a second to remember why he seemed so familiar. Linus, the newcomer she had exchanged numbers with. She felt a little bad – she had completely forgotten to ask Violet if she knew of any businesses that might be hiring. In her defense, she had a lot going on.

"Hi. Linus, right?"

He nodded. "I'm sorry, but I forgot your name. It was a flower of some sort, wasn't it?"

"Flora," she said, smiling. "You were close. How's the job hunt going?"

"I had an interview at the grocery store Saturday," he said. "I'm hoping to get a call back sometime today. I'm going to leave an application here as well, though from how small this place is I'm guessing my chances aren't great. They probably only have a few employees."

"Yeah, I think you're out of luck here. As far as I know, this entire place is run by a family. The woman who owns it, her sister, and some of her in-laws."

"Darn. This really isn't my week." He sighed. "Thanks for the heads up, again."

"No problem. I hope you get that call back from the grocery store. They always seem to be hiring, so your chances are pretty good."

The person in front of her moved, and she turned to walk forward, but Linus said, "Watch out!" His hand landed on her shoulder, holding her back from tripping over a small child who had run out from behind a table at the last moment.

The feeling of his hand on her shoulder made her freeze. His hands were big and heavy, and it reminded her too much of the man who had mugged her. Her breath caught in her throat. Was it possible it had been

Linus? He was new here, needed money, and no one knew anything about him. He was complete stranger – possibly a dangerous one.

His hand slipped off her shoulder a moment later. "Sorry about that. I saw that kid coming out of the corner of my eye."

"No problem," she said, forcing a smile to her face. "Thanks for keeping me from running into him."

"I realize you might be busy with something, but do you want to sit down and eat together? I haven't had a chance to meet many people in town yet."

"Sorry, but I have a busy day ahead of me," she said, barely even pausing to consider his suggestion. The sudden fear that had spiked through her at his touch was enough to erase any sense of sympathy she might have had for him. "I was going to just grab a sandwich to go and eat on my way."

"Gotcha," he said. "Well, it was good to see a friendly face again, at least."

She gave him a tight smile, then stepped forward as the line moved again, grateful that it was her turn to order next.

She didn't know if Linus was the one she should be looking out for or not. All she knew was that she wouldn't be able to trust him until the person who mugged her was behind bars.

As soon as her sandwich was made, she grabbed the bag and hurried back to her truck, locking the doors once she was inside. She knew she wasn't being fair to Linus, and she hoped she would be able to stop being so jumpy soon. She wanted to be able to relax and feel at home in Warbler again, not constantly on her guard.

Instead of eating the sandwich in her truck, she decided to swing by the hardware store and say hi to Grady… and offer him half of her food. Her appetite had been dampened, and she didn't want the sandwich to go to waste.

She parked along the curb in front of the hardware store and stepped inside, her sandwich bag clutched in one hand. She looked over to the counter to say hello to the elderly Mr. Brant, the hardware store's owner, but he was in the middle of a conversation with another customer, a blonde woman who very much did not look like she did her own home repairs, though Flora knew she probably didn't either. She shouldn't judge. She turned her attention to finding Grady instead. He was restocking some hardware in one of the back aisles, but straightened up when he saw her approaching.

"Hey," he said. "What's up?"

"I got my bank card," she told him. "Which means I'm going on a shopping spree. I also brought lunch. Do you have time to take a quick break?"

"Sure," he said, brightening. "Let me just go tell the boss."

She followed him towards the front, hanging back while he approached Mr. Brant and raised his voice to tell the mostly deaf older man that he was going on break. The man nodded and waved him away before turning his attention back to the woman he was still talking to. Flora kept her eyes on her face. She looked familiar – she was sure she had seen her around town before, but she couldn't match her face to a name.

"I can take as long as I want," Grady told her when he returned. "That's his daughter he's talking to. Considering what happened to her ex-husband, they're probably going to be talking for a while."

"She's Phoebe, Ethan's ex-wife?" Flora asked, turning back toward the woman with new consideration. The blonde woman smiled far too brightly for someone who had recently lost someone she used to be close to, and all of a sudden, Flora remembered where she knew her from. This was the same woman who had commented on her choice of the white chocolate caramel latte the day she was mugged.

Officer Hendrick's questions came back to her. He had wanted to know if anyone else knew where she was going, and she had told him Violet was the only one. But that wasn't true, was it? Phoebe had been standing right there. She would have heard Violet say she was going to the nursery to buy some mulch.

But... Flora was certain whoever mugged her was a man. Sure, Violet had thrown out an offhand theory that Phoebe had hired someone to kill her ex-husband, but that didn't explain why she would've hired someone to mug *Flora*. She was jumping to conclusions, and far too quickly. She really was getting paranoid.

Phoebe being at the coffee store the same day Flora was mugged was just a coincidence. Nothing more.

CHAPTER SEVEN

She and Grady split the sandwich in the break room at the hardware store, and since she was already there, she bought a few flowers to add to her garden. They weren't as high quality as the ones at the nursery, but she had already been jumpy and unsettled enough during this trip to town. She didn't need to go back there again alone, not right now.

After that, she went to the grocery store and stocked up on fresh food, relieved to be able to get produce, milk, and other necessities again. Bit by bit, her life was returning to normal. She might have been able to completely move on if it wasn't for Ethan's murder. Even though the only thing tying it to her own mugging was that it had happened on the same day and in the same town, she couldn't shake the feeling that the two were related. It felt wrong for her to move on with her life when a man was dead. She knew, logically, that she couldn't do anything about it, but as she drove home and put her groceries away, she wracked her mind for any faint memory of the incident that might help her figure out who had attacked her. Had Linus's hand on her shoulder felt so frightening because he was the one who attacked her, or was her poor mind just overstressed and making connections where there weren't any? Did Phoebe have anything to do with this at all, or was the woman's presence at the coffee shop and connection to Ethan just another meaningless coincidence?

Having so many questions with no way to answer them was frustrating, but she buried her frustration during her work on the garden. The flowerbeds were really starting to come along. The shed was beginning to look a little better too, she had to admit. She and Grady had finished reinforcing the support beams over the weekend, and were ready to start on the siding.

He came over the next day to help her do just that. He brought some of his own tools over, and the two of them set to work on deconstructing the rotted siding boards on her shed. It was therapeutic to pry the old, rusted nails out and tear the rotted boards away, and by the time they decided to take a break, Flora was sweaty, but happy.

She poured them some lemonade and they sat out on the porch, chatting about anything and everything other than the attack. Flora was glad Grady didn't bring it up. That was one of the differences between him and Violet. They were both great friends in different ways. Violet would push her to talk things through and figure out her feelings, while Grady always seemed to know when she just wanted to be distracted.

"Did Violet invite you to her house on Thursday?" Grady asked her just as she was beginning to brace herself for getting back to work.

"Yeah. It was a group text, which you would know, if you had a cell phone," she said, grinning at him.

He rolled his eyes. "I'll think about it."

"Are you going to the get-together?"

"Yeah," he said. "Don't know what to bring, though. She told me not to bring anything."

"Well, I'm bringing drinks and snacks, and she said she'd cook, so we should be good. You and Sydney are both working that evening; I don't think she wants either of you to feel like you have to make an extra stop before coming over."

"All—" He broke off when a very familiar voice called out to them.

"Yoo-hoo!"

Flora looked away from Grady and down the road to where Beth was approaching with her Basset hound, Sammy, trailing behind her, his droopy ears drooping even further in the heat.

Flora still hadn't told her elderly neighbor that she had been mugged. She felt a little bad about it, because she knew Beth would certainly tell *her* if their positions were reversed, but unlike Grady, Beth never knew when to let anything go. The older woman would mean well, but she would drive Flora up the wall with questions about the mugging and what the police were doing next. She was also prone to gossiping. Right now, no one but her closest friends knew of the attack, and Flora wanted to keep it that way.

"Hi, Flora," Beth said once she drew close enough to talk to them. Flora rose to her feet so she could greet the older woman politely, coming down off the porch steps to give her a quick hug.

"Hi, Beth. How have you been? I haven't seen you around for a while."

Only when she spoke the words did she realize just how long it had been. She hadn't seen Beth for almost a week, and normally, the older woman visited almost every day.

"I'm so sorry for leaving without saying anything, dear," Beth said. Sammy tugged forward on his leash to sniff Flora's legs, and she crouched down to stroke his droopy ears. He was a good dog, even if he seemed to have the energy of a slug. "Tim took a fall, and we had to spend a few days at the hospital. All is well now. I left my phonebook at home, though, and I didn't have your number memorized. I hope you weren't too worried about us."

Flora swallowed against the sudden surge of guilt. She hadn't even noticed until now that the older couple was gone. Sure, she'd had a lot on her mind, but that was no excuse. She might find Beth hard to get along with at times, but she did genuinely like her and her husband. She needed to be a better friend.

"I'm just glad you're okay," she said. "How's Tim doing?"

"He'll be all healed up in a few weeks. It was a hairline fracture on his arm." Beth shook her head. "Listen to my advice, dear. Keep your bones and muscles healthy as you age. You'll appreciate it when you get old."

"I'll keep that in mind," Flora promised.

"I didn't come here to talk about *that*, though," Beth said. "Did you hear what happened in town? We're gone for a few days and people go crazy. Someone was *killed*."

"I heard," Flora said. She hesitated, debating whether or not to bring up her own mugging, but Beth spoke again before she could say anything.

"It's just horrible. This town is changing, and not for the better. I'll bet you anything it was someone who moved here from a big city. Newcomers bring nothing but trouble." She paused and her eyes widened as she realized her error. "Not you, of course, dear. You are such a sweetheart and I'm so glad you moved here."

"That's... good," Flora said, feeling suddenly awkward. "Did you know the man who died?"

"Ethan Alberry? Tim and I have known him for years. He was our tax preparer. He was a very kind man, and I was so glad to hear that he was finally divorcing his wife. She was a nasty piece of work. He deserved someone better. The stories he told about her..." She shook her head. "It's such a shame he passed away before he could find love again."

"I hope the police find out who killed him soon," Flora said.

"Nothing stays secret for long in this town," Beth said. "I'm sure the truth will come out."

"Beth... Since you seem to know him and his wife... do you think there's any way she was involved in what happened to him?"

Beth frowned. "Well, I haven't met the woman. I've only ever heard about her from him. I know she wasn't a kind woman, but I don't know much more than that. I wouldn't feel right saying something unfounded about her, I'm sure you understand. No, my gut tells me this crime is a consequence of the changing times. We've had quite a few people move here from the city over the years, and they bring all sorts of changes with them. Warbler just isn't what it used to be."

Flora took Beth's pronouncement with a grain of salt. Her neighbor was an opinionated lady, and very stuck in her ways. Still, she remembered the feel of Linus's hand on her shoulder, and she didn't dismiss what Beth said completely.

Maybe not all newcomers were bad, but it didn't mean that they were all good, either.

CHAPTER EIGHT

Flora returned to the grocery store Thursday morning in preparation for their get-together that evening. It was nice of Violet to host, not that Flora minded the fact that it usually fell on her shoulders to do so. Violet and Sydney both lived in apartments, with no space for a bonfire, and Grady lived in a trailer she still hadn't even seen. Her house was easily the best option for a group hang-out, and she always enjoyed showing off the progress she had made on it since the last time her friends came over.

It *was* nice not to have to prepare a full meal, though. She grabbed the drinks she knew her friends liked and bought some chips and salsa for snacks, along with a few things she needed at home. Then, she got into line.

It was a long line, the cashier seemed to be moving slowly, so she turned her attention to her cell phone. Her sister had sent her a text message while she was driving to the store, and Flora felt bad reading it.

I miss you! Family dinners just aren't the same. When are you going to visit?

Flora missed her family too. They weren't exactly the closest family in the world – her parents were busy running her father's business and her siblings both led lives of their own, but she usually saw them a few times a month. They had dinners together most Fridays, and always got together for the holidays. Now, it had been months since she had seen any of them.

Still… she had no plans to return to Chicago just yet. She was just so busy. It would take her the better part of the day to drive back up there, and if she wanted to make it worth her time, she would have to stay for a few days, at least. Which meant she would be gone for nearly a week. That meant finding someone to watch her cat for a week, and committing to not doing any work on the house for at least that long too.

She thought she might visit them near the holidays, but that felt like a long time from now. Her aunt was coming to town for Thanksgiving, but Flora still hadn't decided whether she wanted to invite the rest of her family or not. It would be nice to see them, but it would also be… a lot. The line moved forward and Flora tucked her phone away without answering the message yet. She knew she had to make a decision soon. Summer was almost over, the time between now and Thanksgiving would pass quickly.

Someone further up in line complained about how slow it was moving, and Flora glanced at the cashier. She frowned – she recognized the man who was arguing with him. Finn, from the nursery. He was grasping the edge of the counter, his knuckles white.

"You rang it up wrong," he said. "Go back through and do it again. That's way too much for what I'm buying."

"I'm sorry, sir," the man said. "You only have a few items here, and they've all rung up correctly on my screen. Your total is fifty-five eighty-three."

Finn scowled at the cashier. The woman in line between him and Flora said, "If you're just a few dollars short, I have some change I can give you."

"I don't need your charity," he snapped at her. "I just need these useless employees to do their job and ring things up correctly."

His eyes passed over the woman's shoulder and met Flora's. His gaze narrowed, and he turned away from her suddenly.

"You know what? Forget it. I'm out of here."

"Sir, your items," the cashier called out as he walked away, but Finn didn't turn around. He left his cart and his groceries behind and made a beeline for the exit, shoving someone else's cart out of the way angrily.

The woman in front of Flora looked embarrassed. "Oh, dear. I didn't mean to make him walk off in a huff. I was just trying to be nice."

"Just a second," the cashier said. "I need to page someone to take these items back. Sorry for the delay."

The line moved more quickly after that. Flora went through the process of checking out without paying much attention to it. She couldn't shake the feeling that Finn had left when he saw her, specifically, not because he was embarrassed that he couldn't pay. Was he avoiding her because he thought she would recognize him, or was she just being paranoid again?

She paid for her groceries and pushed the cart toward the exit, only for another familiar face to stop her in her tracks. Linus was coming in through the doors and spotted her right away.

"Flora," he called out. "Hey, I didn't expect to see you again so soon. How have you been?"

"I've been good," she told him. "Busy. Have you had any luck with finding a job?"

He grinned. "Yeah, I'm working here now. I'm coming in for my orientation."

"That's good," she said, meaning it. "I knew it would all work out."

"Well, it's no get rich quick scheme, but it'll tide me over. Honestly, I couldn't afford to be too picky. I've been running low on funds. I'm still not sure moving here was the right move, but at least I'm not quite so desperate anymore. My cousin will be glad I'm not just turning around and heading back home, at least."

Had he been desperate enough to mug people? she wondered.

"Well, congratulations," she said. "I'll be seeing you around." It was the only grocery store in town, after all. She was beginning to realize just how cramped Warbler could feel. She couldn't leave her house without running into someone she knew.

"You definitely will," he said. "I'd better get going, I don't want to be late. See you, Flora."

He walked past her and she pushed her cart through the doors. Out of the corner of her eye, she saw someone leaning against the building. Finn. He hadn't left after all, he had just stepped outside. Was he waiting for her? She frowned and shoved her cart forward, but he didn't follow her, though she imagined she could feel his eyes on her back.

She knew Finn had always been grumpy, to the point it had gotten him fired from more than one job, going by what Violet had told her. She knew Linus was probably exactly what he seemed – an innocent man who had moved here for a job that didn't pan out and was looking for a way to make ends meet.

But she also knew she didn't want to be around any of them, or any stranger, until the man who had attacked her was behind bars. She wouldn't be able to stop looking over her shoulder until she knew for sure that the man who mugged her was gone.

CHAPTER NINE

Violet's apartment was shockingly not purple. It was only shocking because of how purple the coffee shop was. The walls were painted a light beige color, and the brightest thing she saw was a dark green couch with a purple throw blanket on it. The apartment was neat and tidy, and Flora always felt a little surprised at just how tame it all was when she visited.

She was greeted at the door with a hug, and dropped the drinks off in Violet's small kitchen.

"See?" her friend said. "You don't *always* have to host get-togethers."

"I really don't mind," Flora said honestly. "But your place is lovely too. I'm always happy to visit."

"I'm glad, I like having people over, even if I don't do it often. Can you keep an eye on the stove timer for me while I freshen up? The lasagna I made will be done soon."

"Of course."

Flora found Violet's oven mitts and pulled the lasagna out of the oven just as another knock sounded on the door. She answered it to find Grady in the hall, and pulled him inside to ogle the lasagna with her. It looked and smelled delicious, and she hadn't eaten since lunch, hours ago. Sydney arrived shortly afterward, and when Violet came out of the restroom she put on some music.

They chatted while they ate. Flora hadn't been aware that this was exactly what she needed. Just an evening with her friends, good food, and a sense of belonging. Once dinner was over, Violet brought out a stack of board games. They started with Monopoly, mostly because Sydney bragged he never lost a game of that.

"You are all cheaters," Violet said when she lost. Sydney had come out on top, as he promised, and Flora had only held on so long because Grady kept trading her the properties she needed. They were terrible trades on his end, but it was a cut-throat game and she wasn't above taking what help she could get. "You're terrible. I don't know why I'm even friends with you."

Flora laughed. "Do you want to play again? We can play a game with teams, and I'll be on yours."

"Girls against guys?" Her friend grinned. "Sure. I'm down for that.

She and Violet won the next game, and Sydney was the one who groaned this time. "I hate boardgames," he complained. "They're only fun when you *don't* lose."

"You're right, it is a lot more fun when you win," Violet said, smug again. She leaned back in the couch, then said, "Oh, Flora. I forgot to tell you. That new guy you were telling me about? He stopped in a few days ago, hoping to put in an application and get hired. I told him I'd take one just in case, but we've got a good team already and don't really need anyone else at the coffee shop for now. I kind of felt bad for him. I was thinking of inviting him along for lunch sometime when we're all getting together so he can start meeting some friendly faces. It sounds like he's had a rough time of it in town."

"I just ran into him at the grocery store today," Flora said. "He got a job there."

"Oh, that's good," Violet said.

"I saw Finn there too," Flora added. "It's weird, I swear he kept glaring at me. I think he was avoiding me, too. When he saw me in line at the cash register, he left all of his purchases behind and left."

"Really?" Violet frowned.

"What reason would he have to avoid you?" Sydney asked.

"That's what I'm wondering," Violet said. "You still haven't heard anything from the police?"

Flora shook her head. "No, and as more time goes on I'm beginning to realize I'm not going to. My stuff is probably gone for good, and unless they catch someone trying to sell my purse or something, the police don't have much to go on."

"I feel like I'm out of the loop," Sydney said. "What does this have to do with some guy at the grocery store giving you the cold shoulder?"

"It's complicated," Flora said, then went on to explain how Finn used to work at the nursery and was recently fired, only a few days before the mugging. "It's a weak connection, but it's all I've got. Though he's not the only one my internal radar keeps sending up red flags about."

She caught them all up on Linus, how overly friendly he had acted toward her, and how she had frozen when he grabbed her shoulder.

"I wonder if I'm just being paranoid," she admitted when she was done. "Everything seems to make me jumpy now."

"Hey, if it keeps you alive, I don't have a problem with it," Violet said. "I've been keeping my ear to the ground to hear if there's been any new news about Ethan's murder, just in case they are related, but I haven't heard anything."

"That's another thing," Flora said. "Phoebe was there the day of the mugging." She told them all about *that*, and realized it was the first time she had gotten everything completely off her chest.

"I don't think Phoebe's the one who mugged me *herself* — it was definitely a man — but if she did have something to do with her husband's death, maybe it's related? I don't know. Sometimes I think I'm going crazy."

"You should trust your gut," Violet told her. "If you think there's something connecting all of this, then I believe you."

"Thanks," she said. "I appreciate it. Being told I'm not completely insane helps more than you know."

It was late by the time things wound down and she decided to head home. She'd fed Amaretto before she left her house, so at least the cat wasn't waiting up for her dinner, but she wasn't used to being up so late anymore.

"I'll walk down with you," Grady volunteered. Down at the car, she gave him a brief hug goodbye. "Are you all right getting home on your own?" he asked. "I can follow you back if you want, make sure you get there safely."

"Thanks, but I'll be all right," she said. "I'm feeling a lot better now, really." And her house was her sanctuary. With the security cameras, she could be sure no one was waiting outside for her, and Grady already did enough for her. He didn't need to do even more.

"All right. I'll see you Sunday. If it doesn't rain, I think we can finish the siding on the shed."

She wasn't looking forward to the work on the shed, exactly, but it would be good to have it done. She estimated they would probably finish by the end of the month, which should be just in time for the coming autumn. It would start raining more soon, and she would be glad to have a repaired shed to put her tools in.

She started her truck and fiddled with the music for a moment until the song she wanted to listen to was playing. Then she pulled out of Violet's parking lot and turned onto the road.

It was always a different experience driving through Warbler at night. The town seemed all but abandoned after a certain time. Chicago never really slept, but after midnight, Warbler turned into a ghost town.

She drove past the hardware store. There was a single car parked across the street from it with its headlights on. She slowed, not sure if it was about to pull out onto the road, but after a moment, the headlights shut off and a woman got out. She froze, recognizing Phoebe. Of course, this was where she lived, wasn't it? Grady had mentioned something about that last week.

Flora passed by her, then looped around the block and parked on the other side of the road, close enough that she could watch as Phoebe unlatched her trunk. She lifted a large suitcase out. Flora could see the tags still attached to the zipper, and from the easy way the woman handled it, it seemed empty.

Another car pulled up behind Violet's and the woman put the suitcase down to wave at the driver before she shut her trunk. A man got out of the second vehicle, and Flora leaned closer to the truck's window, trying to see who it was.

When he turned his face toward a streetlight, she recognized Linus. She inhaled sharply, wondering how he knew Phoebe. He had mentioned something about having a cousin in town, hadn't he? She was sure he had brought it up at least twice, but she hadn't thought to ask who it was. Now, she wished she had.

She watched as he and Phoebe ventured into the apartment building together, the suitcase rolling between them. What was his connection with her? Why had Phoebe purchased a brand-new suitcase? Was she planning on leaving town?

Flora pulled away from the curb with more questions than answers. One in particular followed her all the way home.

What was the job Linus had come to town for? It seemed ridiculous to think of him as a hired killer, but Violet's off-hand remark had stuck with her, and the timing of Linus's arrival to Warbler suddenly seemed a lot more suspicious.

CHAPTER TEN

The connection between Linus and Phoebe bothered Flora all night. She woke up from nightmares about someone grabbing her from behind and demanding her purse, and come morning, she was still tired.

She wished she had asked Linus who his cousin was when he first brought them up in conversation. She still had his number saved on her phone, but she didn't know how to bring the topic up naturally. Even if she *was* his cousin, it didn't necessarily mean anything. He wasn't a hired killer. That was ridiculous. The sleepless nights were getting to her.

She spent the morning painting the entrance hallway, turning her music up louder than usual in an effort to clear her mind. It didn't do much good, but it was better than stewing on her thoughts in silence.

It felt good to finish painting the hallway, at least. She had chosen a pale, natural green, and it made the first steps into her house feel brighter and more welcoming. After washing her painting supplies, she grabbed her to-do list and sat down at the kitchen table to figure out what to tackle next.

It wasn't as if she was running out of things to do – she wanted to repaint all of the walls in the house before she tackled the floors, and that wasn't even mentioning the bigger projects like replacing windows and doors. There was one particular project she kept putting off, though. The ceiling in one of the upper floor bedrooms under where the roof had leaked was warped and crumbling, the drywall on its last legs. She needed to patch it, and she had been watching videos about how to do it for weeks. It was time to stop putting it off. For that, she needed supplies. And that meant another visit to the hardware store.

She made a list of what she thought she needed to buy, though she would double check with Grady to make sure he couldn't think of anything else, then said goodbye to Amaretto and headed into town.

As she slowed and put on her blinker to pull up along the curb in front of the hardware store, her eyes found Phoebe's car, which was still parked in front of her apartment building. She wondered if the other woman was still in her apartment, or if she had absconded during the night with Linus. If she *was* behind the murder, she could be out of the country by now, and Flora was the only one who knew it. She was tempted to call Officer Hendricks, but she suspected she would sound like a crazy person, or worse, a stalker. She didn't have any evidence, after all, and she had spied on the woman just the night before. It might not be illegal to watch someone on a public sidewalk without their knowledge, but it certainly wasn't *normal* either.

Trying to shake the thoughts off, she went inside and raised her voice to greet Mr. Brant. The elderly man waved at her, then gestured toward the entrance to the garden center, already knowing she was there for Grady. She waved at him and continued into the store, grabbing a cart on her way.

Grady was busy loading bags of river stones onto a shelving unit, and she paused to watch his muscles flex as he lifted the heavy bags from the pallet. When he turned to see her, she smiled and walked over.

"I'm ready to start patching my ceiling, and was hoping to get your expertise on the subject," she said. "But it looks like you're busy."

"Let me finish unloading these, then I can take a break," he said. "We got a shipment in this morning. It's been a long day."

"Your back is not going to thank you when you get older."

"That's a concern for older me," he said. He turned back to grab another bag, and Flora crouched down to grab one herself.

"Here, let me help. It's only fair, you help me around the house plenty."

He grunted, but didn't object, and together they finished unloading the pallet before he stretched and leaned against the shelving unit.

"All right, what do you need?"

She withdrew her list. "I think this is everything I'll need to patch the ceiling, but I'm basing it off of a few instructional videos I saw. Is there anything I'm missing?"

He looked over the list. "Looks like you've got everything you'll need, but grab some particle masks as well. Drywall is dusty and you don't want to breathe it in."

She nodded and took the list back. "Thanks. Do you think I'm getting ahead of myself? Can I do this on my own?"

"Of course," he said, not sounding doubtful in the least. "Just take your time and if you have any doubts, call for help or look up what you need online. Drywall is a pain to work with, but it's not hard as long as you're patient and take your time."

"Thanks," she said. "I think you have more faith in me than I do in myself."

He snorted. "Come on, let's find what you need."

They entered into the main part of the store, Flora pushing her cart ahead of her. She was familiar enough with the store by now that she didn't really need Grady's help to find what she needed, but it was always nice to chat with him while she shopped, and he always had advice about what brands to buy and which to avoid.

The drywall itself was in the back, and he told her he would bring it out and load it into the truck for her while she paid. Once her cart was full, she headed to the register. Grady paused to talk to Mr. Brant so he could ring the drywall up for her, then vanished into the back to fetch it.

Flora put her items on the counter and waited while the elderly man typed in each number by hand. Checking out was never a speedy business unless Grady was at the register, but Flora didn't mind. It was hardly like she was in a hurry.

The door to the hardware store opened and Flora looked up. Phoebe strode inside, and Flora's first thought was *Well, I guess she hasn't fled the country yet.* Her next thought was how tired the woman looked. She had dark bags under her eyes, and wore none of the makeup Flora had seen her with before.

"Dad," she said. "Dad!"

It took her almost shouting for Mr. Brant to hear her. "Phoebe," he said, turning toward her. "Why are you here?"

"I'm leaving today," she said, half-shouting at him. "I wanted to say goodbye."

She glanced at Flora, but there wasn't any recognition in her gaze. It made her wonder if her suspicion of the other woman was wrong. If Phoebe didn't even recognize her, what were the chances she had anything to do with the mugging?

"You're leaving already?" Mr. Brant said. "I thought that was tomorrow."

"I told you yesterday. I'll see you later, Dad. I'm not sure when I'll be back."

She stepped around the counter and gave him a hug, her movements brusque and impatient.

"Have a good trip," her father said. "Be careful. You're leaving right now?"

"I told you I was leaving this afternoon. I have to finish loading the car, then I'm going to go grab a coffee for the road, then I'm out of here. I'll call you, okay? Take care of yourself, Dad."

Then, with another glance at Flora, she stepped away and pushed through the door, leaving as suddenly as she had come. Mr. Brant gazed after her for a moment, frowning, then returned to ringing up Flora's items.

Flora watched through the window as Phoebe walked back across the road. The other woman *was* leaving town. She felt validated – her impromptu investigation the night before had given her one good clue, at least. She still didn't know *why*, or whether Linus was connected or not, and she wasn't ever going to get answers to those questions unless she hurried. Violet Delights was the only decent coffee shop in town. If Phoebe wanted to get coffee on her way to wherever she was going, she would be stopping there.

While Mr. Brant continued to ring up her items, she got her money out so she would be ready to pay. If she hurried, she might be able to get to the coffee store first and figure out a way to get answers to her questions. Violet was the one who had told her how much Phoebe hated her husband. She was sure her friend would agree to help her get the answers she wanted.

CHAPTER ELEVEN

Grady was just closing her truck's tailgate when Flora left the hardware store. She hurried past him and pulled the driver's door open to toss her bags onto the passenger's seat.

"Thanks," she called out to him. "Sorry for the rush, but I've got to go talk to Violet about something."

"Good luck on the ceiling," he called out as she started her truck. "Let me know if you need help."

She waved at him, then shut her door and checked the mirror before pulling out onto the road, heading straight for the coffee shop. Phoebe had vanished, presumably going up to her apartment to finish packing, so Flora had time to beat her to Violet Delights.

She parked in the first spot she saw across the street from the coffee shop, and waited for the traffic to clear enough that she could cross safely. The familiar, warm scent of coffee and sugar wrapped around her as she walked inside. There were a few people sitting at the tables, but no one was in line, and Violet looked up from her phone when she came in.

The other woman smiled, standing up to greet Flora.

"Hey. Your normal latte again?"

Flora shook her head, then hesitated and nodded. She could use a pick-me-up. "Yes, actually, but that's not what I'm here for." She lowered her voice. "Phoebe is about to come in. She's going on a trip. And I think she knows Linus – look, it's a long story, but you think you could try to figure out where she's going?"

Violet blinked, but took her request in stride. "Sure. I'll try to make it sound natural." She narrowed her eyes. "Do you really think she has something to do with the murder? I know what I said, but I don't know the woman from Eve myself. It was just something I heard from a friend."

Flora shrugged. "I'm not sure of anything, but what you said stuck with me. I think… I think she's Linus's cousin, and the reason he came to town. And Linus arrived in town right around when the mugging and murder happened. There's got to be something there. My gut tells me something more is going on."

"All right. How about I don't start making your coffee until she comes in? That will give you an excuse to stand up here near the counter while she orders."

"Perfect," Flora said. "Thanks, Violet. I appreciate it."

"Hey, I'm all for helping you out with your investigation as long as it's not actually dangerous."

Flora smiled. "Thanks. I owe you." She frowned. "I hate being so jumpy all the time. I'd almost rather run into the person who attacked me again, just so I can know who it is and can stop worrying all the time. Does that sound weird?"

"Super weird," Violet said cheerfully. "But I understand, or at least I think I do. Sometimes worrying about something is worse than having it actually happen."

Flora nodded. "Exactly."

She stayed by the counter, chatting with her friend until the bell above the door jingled and Phoebe came in. She looked just as harried as she had at the hardware store, and didn't even glance at Flora.

"Can I get an iced vanilla latte, with a double shot of espresso?" she asked Violet as she made a beeline for the counter.

"Coming right up," Violet said, beginning to work on Flora's drink. "There's just one person ahead of you. Sounds like you're expecting to have a busy day."

Phoebe frowned and glanced over at Flora for the first time. Her brows furrowed. She might not have recognized her at the hardware store, but she certainly seemed to register that she'd seen Flora just a few minutes before.

"I'm heading out of town," she said slowly.

"Oh?" Violet asked as she frothed Flora's latte. "Anywhere interesting?"

"I'm heading out to New Hampshire to visit my mom. I've had enough of Warbler for a while."

Flora and Violet exchanged a look as Violet spread whipped cream on top of the latte.

"What was that?" Phoebe snapped. They both looked over at her, to see she was scowling. "You two keep glancing at each other. Did you plan this?"

"I don't know what you're talking about," Violet said, handing Flora's latte over and grabbing another cup to start on Phoebe's drink.

"You were just at the hardware store, and you heard me tell my dad about my trip," Phoebe said, staring at Flora. "And now *she's* asking me all about it. You two are just like everyone else. I cannot catch a *break.* For the last time, I didn't have anything to do with what happened to Ethan. Yes, I divorced him, yes he drove me up the wall, yes I've said some unfortunate things in the past, but no, I didn't get him murdered. *This* is why I'm leaving. Warbler is a terrible place to be right now. I can't believe even the woman who makes my coffee is attacking me now."

Violet and Flora exchanged another glance. "I'm sorry," Violet said. "I didn't mean to upset you."

"Sorry?" Phoebe said. "Sorry isn't good enough. I am sick to death of this. I was supposed to spend this past week helping my cousin get settled in and celebrating his new job, instead, I've been getting harassed and harried from every angle because a man I don't have anything to do with anymore was killed."

"Is Linus your cousin?" Flora asked.

Phoebe glared at her. "Yes, he is my cousin. How do you know him?"

"We ran into each other a few times," Flora said. "I'm glad he found a new job. I'm sorry for making you uncomfortable, it wasn't my intention."

"New job?" Phoebe asked, ignoring her apology. "What are you talking about? He had a job lined up before he moved here."

Flora frowned. "It fell through. Didn't he tell you about it?"

"I have no idea what you're talking about. He would've told me if his job fell through."

"Look, we're sorry for cornering you like this," Violet said. "The coffee is on the house today. I hope you have a good time on your trip."

"Thank you," the woman said, her voice tight. "Everything about this town just keeps getting worse and worse."

Still muttering to herself, Phoebe took her coffee and left. Flora accepted her own drink from Violet and the two of them exchanged a muted look. "Sorry," Flora said. "I feel bad. I shouldn't have involved you like that."

"No, it's okay," her friend said. "I volunteered to help you. It's not your fault. I just… I feel bad. If she really is innocent, it must be horrible for her to go through all of this. I really need to learn to keep my mouth shut when I'm not sure about something."

"Do you think I should go apologize to her?" Flora asked.

"I don't know if it would help," Violet said. "I just hope I haven't lost her business for good. She's not exactly a regular, but I don't want to drive anyone away."

"I'll go talk to her," Flora decided. "I'll at least explain it wasn't your fault. You didn't have anything to do with it. You were just helping me."

Feeling confident in her choice, she paid Violet for the coffee – both coffees, despite her friend's protests – and went back outside. She still wasn't sure how she felt about Phoebe. The woman had seemed truly upset, but it could have been an act. Apologizing would hopefully help Violet, at least.

She took a step toward Phoebe's car, then paused. The other woman wasn't in it. Flora looked up and down the sidewalk, but she had vanished. She wasn't across the street, and the neighboring business was an insurance office – not exactly somewhere someone who was about to leave town would go.

"Phoebe?" she called out.

From the alley next to the coffee shop, someone screamed.

CHAPTER TWELVE

Flora ran toward the scream before her mind could catch up to what her body was doing. She wasn't brave, not really, but she also wasn't the sort of person who could run away from someone who was in trouble.

She rounded the corner of the coffee shop and froze mid-step. Phoebe was there, but she wasn't alone. A large man wearing a black ski mask and black gloves was standing behind her. He had one arm around her throat, and a knife was in his other hand. Flora's heart thundered in her chest. A part of her could still feel his hands on her, and her body remembered every moment of the terror she had faced. She tried to say something, to tell him to stop or else she would call the police, but the words wouldn't come out. Her lungs seemed to have frozen solid in her chest.

"Help me!" Phoebe cried out. "He's going to kill me!"

"Just drop your purse," the man said. "And you, get out of here. Or she loses her life."

"Let me go," Phoebe said, struggling. "I'm not giving you anything."

He brought the knife up to her neck. "I'm not playing around. If you try to fight me, I will do it. You must have heard about that man who was murdered. That was me. I did that because he thought he could fight me. I'm not playing around. Give me your purse. Right now."

Flora saw Phoebe's throat move as she gulped. "No! I'm not giving you anything."

"Wait!" Flora, but she was too slow.

Phoebe stomped down on the man's foot. He cursed and jerked back, bringing the knife down to her shoulder. Flora saw blood and she screamed, glad that her lungs were working again, at the very least.

Phoebe fell down with a shout, but before she could get away, the man grabbed her hair.

"Leave her be!" Flora shouted. She was still terrified, but she couldn't stand the thought of watching Phoebe *die* right in front of her. She saw the man reach down to pull Phoebe back up, and forced her legs to move. She felt like she was moving in a dream, but somehow she was close enough to push the man back before he got a good grip on the other woman.

He stumbled back and brought the knife up. She yanked her arms back just in time. Out of the corner of her eye, she saw Phoebe climb to her feet.

"*You* killed Ethan?" she spat. "I might have *said* I wished he would drop dead, but I didn't *mean* it. There is no way I'm going to get stabbed by the same guy who killed him."

"All I wanted was your purse," the man snapped. "It didn't have to end like this."

Flora was close enough to see his eyes narrow through the holes in the mask. Her heart skipped a beat in her chest. He wasn't disguising his voice anymore, but that wasn't what tipped her off. No, it was the way he glared at them. She had seen that same glare directed at her just days ago.

It wasn't Linus after all. She had been wrong about him, and about Phoebe.

"Finn?" she blurted out.

His eyes widened slightly, and his grip on the knife tightened. "That's it, then. Neither of you can get away now."

He lunged for her, and Phoebe screamed as Flora stumbled back. Her reflexes must have improved with all of the physical labor she had been doing, because if she was just a hair slower, he would have grabbed her.

She heard footsteps behind her and realized Phoebe was running away. She was alone in the alley with him, standing just out of reach of his knife. They stood there in silence for a moment, both of them breathing heavily.

"You know, I always hated carrying those stupid, heavy bags of mulch. Stealing your purse felt like revenge for that."

"You went from petty theft to murder in a matter of hours," Flora said. "I'm glad Ms. Michaels fired you. You've been a monster all along."

"You don't know anything about me. Don't act like you do."

"Was it worth it?" she asked, figuring that as long as he was talking, he wasn't stabbing her. "Did you get anything from Ethan that made it worth killing him? Ending a life?"

"I didn't think it would go so far, but I don't regret it. I should have been more careful, but getting your purse was so easy." He chuckled. "He thought he could fight me off, but I was ready for it. It happened so quickly, I barely had time to enjoy the feeling of finally putting someone in their place. I should have killed you too, that first time. When I saw you at the grocery store, I couldn't believe how *normal* you looked. You should have been afraid of me! I'm going to force all of these idiots around town to respect me. It's time that I get what I deserve around here, instead of hopping from one crappy job to the next because people are too close-minded to work alongside anyone who isn't a smiling dolt."

Flora took advantage of his rant to force her feet back into motion. She was already running out of the alley when he lunged for her. Her feet pounded across concrete and then asphalt as she ran into the road. Someone honked at her, but she didn't slow down. She could hear Finn's steps right behind her.

The coffee shop was *right there*, but she didn't want to bring a knife-wielding maniac into Violet's shop. The other woman had already been inadvertently involved in all of this, and Flora didn't want to risk her getting hurt. She wove between cars parked along the curb instead, glad for the attention they were drawing, not that she wanted a bystander to step in and get hurt either. The more people saw what was happening, the higher the chances that someone would call the police. She kept hoping she would hear the chirp of a police siren, but she had no such luck. She was on her own for this.

At least, she thought she was. She looked around when she heard a horn honk, and saw Phoebe's car sitting in the middle of the road. She ran toward it and yanked the passenger door open, falling inside and pulling it shut just as Finn collided with the vehicle. He pounded on the window.

"I'll hunt you both down," he threatened. He slammed the hilt of the knife into the glass, but it held. "I'm going to kill you!"

"Oh my gosh," Phoebe said. She pressed on the gas pedal too hard, sending them careening forward. "Is this really happening?"

"Just drive," Flora said. "Go to the police station. Even if he doesn't catch us, he might attack someone else."

Phoebe didn't argue with that. She sped through town while Flora shifted around to pull her cell phone from the pocket of her jeans. Officer Hendricks was going to have a conniption fit when he heard what she was involved in, but she didn't care. He could mutter about her absurdly bad luck all he wanted as long as he arrested Finn before he hurt someone else.

EPILOGUE

"I still can't believe you thought I was the murderer," Linus said, "but I guess I can't blame you."

It had been nearly a week since her encounter with Finn, and it was her first time seeing Linus since. She leaned back against the grocery store's wall, next to a selection of potato chips.

"Sorry about that," she said. "I wasn't doing very well at the time. The whole mugging thing had me pretty jumpy."

"Oh, I don't blame you at all," he told her. "I just feel bad if I frightened you."

"There's no way you could have known," she told him. "I'm curious, though, why didn't you tell Phoebe the job you moved here for didn't pan out?"

"I should have," he admitted. "She's the one who sent me the job listing, and I thought if she knew how much having the job offer pulled out from under me at the last second screwed my life up, she would feel bad. I was planning on telling her as soon as I had settled in here at the grocery store."

"I really should have taken you up on that offer to eat lunch together," Flora said with a sigh. "I might have realized I was mistaken about you and Phoebe."

"I'm a little flattered you thought I was a hired killer," he admitted, chuckling. "But I'm glad everything is straightened out now."

"I still feel really bad," Flora admitted. "Thanks for being so easygoing about everything."

"This move definitely didn't go how I expected it to," he said. "But things are looking up now, at least."

"Speaking of you being new to town," Flora said. "I'm having some people over Friday night. My friend Violet, from the coffee shop – I think you met her, a guy named Grady, and Sydney. I know you haven't met very many people yet. Would you like to come over? Grady is going to be picking up a grill for me, so we'll be cooking out. It should be fun and laid-back. They're a good group of people."

"Yeah, I'd love to come," he said. "You still have my number?" She nodded. "Just text me your address, then. It will be nice to meet some more people."

"Trust me, I know how it is," she said. "I'm new here too. Things got a lot easier once I had some friends I could rely on. Just give it a few months, and you'll feel as at home in town as I do."

She didn't want to get him in trouble with his new boss for chatting while he was supposed to be working, so she pushed away from the wall and said goodbye before she continued shopping. Ever since Finn was arrested, she had felt much better about coming into town, though the experience had shaken her. Finn was a normal man, one who had spent most of his life here in Warbler. Desperation and resentment had driven him to do horrible things. It was an unpleasant reminder that crime could exist anywhere, in any community.

But life continued. She had a cart full of fresh produce, a freshly repaired ceiling in the upstairs bedroom, and the shed was well on its way to getting a second chance at life. She had her friends, she had a family who loved her, and she had a future that she looked forward to. It would take time to leave the bad memories behind, but she would hold on to the good ones forever.

Made in the USA
Coppell, TX
23 October 2023

23271512R00069